SCARLETT AND SAM

ESCAPE FROM EGYPT

by Eric A. Kimmel

illustrations by Ivica Stevanovic

KAR-BEN
PUBLISHING

Text copyright © 2015 by Eric A. Kimmel
Illustrations copyright © 2015 by Lerner Publishing Group

The image in this book is used with the permission of: © Vitaly Korovin/
Shutterstock.com, (sand).

KAR-BEN PUBLISHING
An imprint of Lerner Publishing Group, Inc.
241 First Avenue North
Minneapolis, MN 55401 USA
1-800-4-KARBEN

Website address: www.karben.com

Main body text set in Janson Text LT Std.
Typeface provided by Adobe Systems.

Library of Congress Cataloging-in-Publication Data

Kimmel, Eric A.
    Scarlett and Sam : escape from Egypt / by Eric A. Kimmel ;
illustrated by Ivica Stevanovic.
       pages   cm
    Summary: Grandma Mina's Persian carpet sends twins Scarlett and
Sam to Egypt in the time of Moses, where they come to understand
that every Jew was part of the first Passover and just what made it
different from all other nights.
    ISBN 978-1-4677-3850-7 (lib. bdg. : alk. paper)
    ISBN 978-1-4677-6207-6 (eBook)
    [1. Time travel—Fiction. 2. Passover—Fiction. 3. Jews—Fiction.
4. Brothers and sisters—Fiction. 5. Twins—Fiction. 6. Egypt—
History—Eighteenth dynasty, ca. 1570-1320 B.C.—Fiction. 7. Bible.
Old Testament—History of Biblical events—Fiction.] I. Stevanovic,
Ivica, illustrator. II. Title.
PZ7.K5648Sc 2015
[Fic]—dc23   2013044269

Manufactured in China
2-53578-15960-6/12/2022

0323/B2142/A8

CONTENTS

CHAPTER 1
THE CARPET

Sam and Scarlett were twins. They had the same dark hair and green eyes, the same chins, ears, and noses. They sounded alike. They were even the same height and weight. They were best friends too. But sometimes they liked to argue.

Tonight was one of those times.

It was the first night of Passover. Sam and Scarlett were going to help to lead the family Seder. Who would ask the Four Questions? That part always went to the youngest child at the table. Sam and Scarlett shared the same birthday. This was not going to be easy.

"I want to do it," said Sam.

"Well, so do I!" said Scarlett.

"Why don't you read the questions together like you did last year?" suggested their dad.

"No way! I'm not doing that again," Scarlett said. "Last year was a mess. Sam reads too slowly."

"Well, you read too fast," Sam shot back. "I have an idea. Why don't we divide up the questions? I'll take the first two. You take the last two."

"No! You take the last two. The first two questions are the best. Everybody knows that."

Sam rubbed his forehead. "Here we go again. Come on, Scarlett! Quit trying to take the best parts for yourself."

That's when Grandma Mina got into the act. She stood up from her seat on the other end of the table. Grandma Mina had grown up in Iran. Her flowing gown and colorful scarf matched the colors and patterns of the Persian carpet that hung on the dining room wall behind her.

The carpet was hundreds of years old. It was the only thing Grandma Mina brought with her when her family had to leave their home. They left everything behind—but not that carpet.

"The carpet is woven with magic," Grandma Mina always said. "It has been part of our family throughout the ages. If only that carpet could talk. What stories it could tell!"

Right now, Grandma Mina wasn't looking for stories. She was looking for quiet.

"Sam and Scarlett!" She clapped her hands to get their attention. Sam and Scarlett stopped squabbling.

"Listen to me, both of you. It doesn't matter which of you asks the Four Questions. The answers are what matter. Tonight, at the Seder, we don't just tell the story of Passover. We become part of it. You, I—all the Jewish people all over the world. We all take part in the Passover story. We were there. It happened to each of us."

"Huh?" said Sam. "That doesn't make sense, Grandma. The first Passover happened in Egypt three thousand years ago. Nobody alive was there then."

"You're wrong," Grandma Mina said. "We were all there. The whole Jewish people. In every land, in every age. We *all* were in Egypt *together*."

"You mean Sam and me?" said Scarlett. "We weren't even born then!"

Grandma Mina turned to the carpet on the wall. "Look at the carpet. Can you see how it is made of different threads? Thousands of threads, all dyed different colors. Yet they are still part of the same design. So it is with us. We are all part of this story. Like the threads of the carpet. All of us together...in Egypt...then...and now."

That's when something odd began to happen.

Grandma Mina's voice faded. Hot winds began to blow. Scarlett and Sam stared at the carpet. It began to shimmer. Colors swirled before their eyes.

"What's going on?" cried Scarlett. "I feel dizzy."

"Me too!" said Sam.

The twins held tightly to each other as a powerful force pulled them toward the carpet.

"What's happening?" Scarlett shouted. "Sam, don't let go! Stay with me!"

"I'm trying!" Sam yelled back. Loud whooshing sounds drowned out their voices. The room turned black. The whoosh became a roar. The twins felt as if they were flying backwards through the air. They held on to each other as the carpet bucked and bumped through space.

The air around them felt icy cold. Then it began to grow warm. Warmer and warmer until it

turned...HOT!

The carpet came down with a thud. Its colors faded, then vanished. Sam and Scarlett bounced and rolled. Something soft and gritty cushioned their fall.

"Whoa! That was some ride!" said Scarlett, brushing herself off.

"Where are we?" said Sam. "Where's the carpet?"

"Your guess is as good as mine," said Scarlett. She picked up a handful of sand. It was almost too hot to hold. "Sand? How did we get to the beach?"

"I don't think this is a beach," said Sam. "There isn't any water."

"Then what's with all this sand?" said Scarlett.

The blazing sun beat down on them. All at once, they realized the answer to that question.

"We're in the desert!" they said together.

CHAPTER 2
IN THE DESERT

It was a desert, all right.

Sam and Scarlett found themselves surrounded by an ocean of sand. No matter where they looked, they saw the same thing. Miles and miles of empty, glaring white sand. "How did we get here?" asked Scarlett.

"Grandma Mina's carpet must have brought us," said Sam. "She always said it was special. I guess she wasn't just talking about its pretty colors."

Sam felt his lips cracking. Scarlett's eyes felt hot and dry. Blinking didn't help. It only made her eyes feel drier and scratchier.

"I wish I had my sunglasses," Scarlett said.

"And sunscreen," Sam added. "Do you see a drugstore?"

"No, but I see something else," said Scarlett. She pointed to three triangles rising above the sand dunes. "Aren't those pyramids?"

Sam squinted into the sun. "They're shaped like pyramids," he said. "But these things are white. Aren't the pyramids supposed to be a sandy color? Like Dad's khaki pants?"

Scarlett didn't answer. She was staring at a crouching animal statue in front of the pyramids. "I don't know about that," said Scarlett. "But if those *are* pyramids, that must be the Sphinx!"

"But the Sphinx doesn't have all those colors," said Sam. "Unless somebody painted it."

"And gave it a nose. And a beard." Scarlett pointed to the long, skinny beard on the Sphinx's chin. "Not a good idea. It looks kind of goofy."

"This is all kind of goofy," said Sam. "The carpet must've dropped us into the middle of some weird theme park."

"Well, let's start looking for the exit," Scarlett said. "And a refreshment stand. I'm so thirsty that I might turn to sand myself if I don't get something to drink soon."

"I could use a restroom," said Sam. "I really have to go."

"Look around. Maybe you can find a tree."

"It's a desert. There aren't any trees. I don't even see a cactus."

"Well, go behind that sand dune," Scarlett suggested. "I promise not to look."

Sam raced up the sand dune. He disappeared on the other side. Scarlett waited for him to come back.

And waited.

And waited.

And waited.

Scarlett began to worry. She knew she'd promised not to look. But Sam might be in trouble. She began climbing the sand dune. Her feet slipped on the burning hot sand. Scratchy grains got inside her shoes. She felt hot and thirsty and totally miserable.

"Whatever this place is, I hate it," Scarlett mumbled to herself.

After climbing and slipping for several minutes, Scarlett reached the top of the dune. She looked down. Far away on the other side, she saw Sam. But he wasn't alone. He was talking to two rough-looking men. The men wore weird-looking striped hats that looked like grocery bags and covered their necks and shoulders. The only other clothes they had on looked like baggy swimming trunks that came down to their knees. Could they be surfers? If they were surfers, where was the beach? It sure didn't look like there was any surf within a thousand miles of this place.

"Sam!" Scarlett yelled. She waved her arms to catch his attention. Sam looked up. So did the surfers. Sam waved his arms back at Scarlett. He began yelling something. But Scarlett was too far away to make out what he was saying. She moved forward to hear him better. That's when one of the men grabbed Sam's arm. The other one began racing up the dune. "This doesn't look good," Scarlett said to herself. "He's coming after me..."

What should she do? Stay with Sam? Run for help? Where? She hadn't seen any police cars drive by. Meanwhile, that surfer dude was getting closer. Hot sand didn't seem to slow him down. He was nearly at the top of the dune.

Scarlett got a better look at him now. This dude was definitely not a surfer! Those were not swim trunks. He was wearing some sort of pleated kilt around his middle. His hat wasn't a hat at all. It was a wig. The hair was braided into tight, thin braids held together with wire and beads. Worst of all was what she saw in his hand: a nasty-looking whip!

Scarlett knew what she had to do.

She took off.

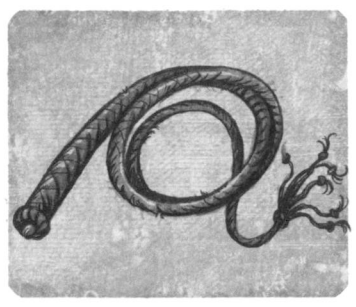

CHAPTER 3
PRISONERS

She didn't get far. Her feet slipped in the sand. Down she went. Scarlett rolled head over heels to the bottom of the dune. The man grabbed her arm. He yanked her to her feet.

Scarlett had sand in her hair, in her shoes, in her mouth and eyes. "Let me go!" she yelled. "Or I'll...I'll..." Scarlett wanted to make a threat, but she couldn't think of anything threatening. Finally, she said, "I'll tell my dad."

It wasn't much of a threat. It didn't work.

"Watch how you speak to me, slave!" the man answered. "Did you think you could escape? Where did you think you could run? There's nothing here but sand." He laughed long and hard. "You're lucky. I'm in a good mood. Otherwise, I would give you a taste of this."

He cracked the whip.

Scarlett gulped.

The man marched her back up the dune. He cracked the whip every few yards to hurry her along. It was the same going down the other side. Scarlett slid most of the way to the bottom.

When she got there, she saw Sam. The other man held him by the collar.

"We're in trouble," whispered Sam as the men marched them toward the pyramids.

"Duh!" said Scarlett. "But don't worry. I've got my cell phone in my pocket. I'll wait till they're not looking. Then I'll call 911."

"I don't think that'll work," Sam said. "You won't get a signal here."

"Why not?" Scarlett asked.

"They don't have cell phone towers in ancient Egypt."

"Ancient Egypt?" Scarlett gasped. "What are we doing in ancient Egypt?"

"Grandma Mina's carpet brought us back in time," said Sam. "I figured it out while I was trying to ask those guys for directions. That's why the pyramids look strange. In ancient Egypt they were covered with white stone. They only turned that sandy color a thousand years later, when people pulled off the stone to build houses. And the Sphinx was painted. It had a red face and a blue beard. Take a look at it. Red face. Blue beard. Am I right?"

"The evidence seems to back you up," Scarlett admitted. "How do you know all this stuff?"

"I saw it on The History Channel."

"Keep moving! No talking!" The man who captured Scarlett stopped their conversation with a crack of his whip. *SNAP!* He cracked it again—right next to Scarlett's ear.

"Hey, watch it!" cried Scarlett. "There are laws against child abuse."

"Not here," said Sam as he and Scarlett stumbled across the burning hot sand.

***

The two Egyptians forced the twins to climb one enormous dune after another. The hot sand scorched their feet. Sweat dripped down their faces. Just when they thought they couldn't take another step, they reached the top of the last dune. Looking down, they saw a road. Sam and Scarlett couldn't wait to reach it. Walking on flat ground had to be way easier than struggling over hot, slippery dunes.

But before the twins could go any farther, they saw a disturbing sight: a long line of people pulling an enormous statue along the road. From the top of the dune, the people looked like ants lugging a big piece of candy back to their nest. The immense statue had to be taller than Sam and Scarlett's house. The people tugged on ropes tied around the statue. All of them were covered with dust. Their clothes were rags. They looked thin and hungry, as if they hadn't had a good meal in a long, long time. Except for the two dozen guys with whips, who strutted up and down the line of struggling people. *They* sure didn't look as if they had missed any meals. Sam and Scarlett saw one guy crack his whip across a worker's back.

"This is terrible!" Scarlett exclaimed. "Why should those poor, weak people have to pull that huge statue in this heat?"

"They must be slaves," Sam said. "Remember how our new friend here called you a slave earlier?"

"Of course I remember! But I still can't believe what I'm seeing. What gives those Egyptians the right to be so cruel?"

Sam didn't have an answer to that question. And he didn't have time to think of one before the twins' Egyptian captors started pushing them down the dune and onto the road.

Another Egyptian slave driver walked up to look them over. This man was huge and scary. He carried a long, black whip—longer and nastier-looking than any of the others Sam and Scarlett had seen so far.

"We found some strays," said the Egyptian who'd chased down Scarlett.

"Actually, I think there's been a misunderstanding," said Sam. "We're not slaves. We're not even from around here. We're just trying to get home..."

"Are you Hebrews?" demanded the slave driver with the monster whip.

Sam and Scarlett looked at each other.

"Why is he asking if we're Jewish?" Scarlett whispered.

"I don't know," Sam said. "Maybe he's wondering if we need a kosher meal."

"Yeah," they answered proudly. "We are Hebrews."

The man snapped his whip. "Then GET TO WORK!"

CHAPTER 4
GOOD NEWS

CRACK!

The Egyptian's whip flashed an inch from Sam's nose.

"These guys mean business," Sam whispered to Scarlett as they hurried to join the other slaves.

"You bet they do," one of the slave boys said. "Best keep your mouth closed. They don't put up with any whining or complaining."

"Why are they so mean?" Scarlett asked.

"The Egyptians are building two cities, Pithom and Ramses," the boy answered. "Pharaoh wants them finished by his birthday."

"When's his birthday?" Sam asked.

"Next month. The work isn't even half done."

"The Egyptians will finish on time—if it kills us!" another slave added.

"Quiet!" barked the slave driver. "Less talk, more work! Get busy, you two!" The whip snapped again. It flicked up the sand at the twins' feet. They had to dance to keep the whip's tail from stinging their skin.

Sam and Scarlett grabbed hold of one of the ropes and pulled with the other slaves.

They pulled.

And pulled.

And pulled.

The statue barely budged. That wasn't surprising. The Egyptians had invented the chariot, but they still hadn't figured out the wagon.

The statue was being pulled along on rollers made from logs. When one log reached the back of the statue's pedestal, slaves would pick it up. They would carry it to the front to be used again.

"This is so inefficient," Sam whispered to Scarlett.

"That's the least of our worries," Scarlett whispered back.

For what seemed like hours, frightened slaves pulled on ropes. Other slaves ran around with heavy logs on their shoulders, trying not get crushed as they placed the rollers in front of the moving statue. Meanwhile, the Egyptians kept cracking their whips, lashing anyone who didn't work hard enough.

"This is a nightmare! Why doesn't someone say something?" Sam murmured.

"It's like kids who are bullied at school," said Scarlett. "Someone needs to show them how to stand up for themselves. These slaves can't do it.

They're too scared. If someone's going to do anything about it, it has to be us."

"Please! Don't say anything," a slave girl pleaded. "You'll only make the Egyptians angry. That will make it worse for all of us."

"How can it get worse than this?" Sam asked. He pulled the rope as hard as he could.

"You don't know the Egyptians," the slave girl whispered. "They can always think of new ways to make our lives even more miserable."

"And after we finish today, we still have to make bricks," said a slave boy.

"Bricks?" Scarlett echoed.

"Each slave has to make fifty bricks per day. The Egyptians count them. If there aren't enough bricks, we have to make more. If there are too many, the count has to begin all over again. It's usually long past dark by the time we finish. Then they give us a handful of grain for our supper. We still have to grind it and bake it. Finally, we get to sleep for a few hours, if we're lucky. When the sun comes up, we start working again."

"Don't you get any time off?" Scarlett asked. "Weekends? Holidays? Shabbat?"

"Time off? What's that?" the slave girl asked.

"You've got to be kidding!" Sam exclaimed.

"I can't believe it! No holidays!" Scarlett said.

"Believe it!" a slave boy said. "It was bad enough when the Egyptians still gave us straw to put in the bricks. All we had to do was dig the clay and mix in the straw. Then this guy named Moses showed up. Something he said made Pharaoh angry. Pharaoh's afraid to touch Moses, so he took it out on us. Now we have to wander around in the fields after dark, trying to find our own straw. It takes forever. But we still have to make as many bricks as before."

"That's not fair!" said Scarlett.

"There's nothing fair about being a slave," an old man replied.

"Scarlett, did you hear that?" Sam whispered. "That slave boy talked about Moses. Moses is here. Now. In Egypt."

"That means the time of freedom can't be far away!" said Scarlett.

"Right," said Sam. "Plus, if anyone can help us get home, it's Moses!"

"What makes you think that?" asked Scarlett.

"He's a prophet, Scarlett! He's one of our greatest teachers. He'll figure something out."

"Then let's start looking for him," Scarlett said.

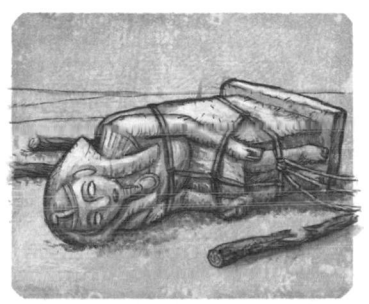

CHAPTER 5

MOSES AND AARON

"We won't find Moses here, that's for sure," Scarlett went on. "We have to find a way to escape."

"But how can we do that?" said Sam. "There are Egyptians everywhere. They're stronger than we are. They're watching us all the time. We'll never get away."

"Just be patient," Scarlett said. "We'll wait for them to get distracted. Then we'll run."

The twins kept working. The burning desert sun rose higher in the sky. As hours passed, Sam and Scarlett became hotter, hungrier, and thirstier. Pulling on the rope gave them blisters. They were so tired that they could barely move.

Suddenly Sam and Scarlett heard a loud *CRACK!* The towering statue swayed forward.

"Look out!" a slave yelled.

"One of the rollers broke!" shouted another slave. "The statue's falling over!"

Sam and Scarlett quickly saw what was happening. One of the thick logs being used to move the statue had snapped under its weight. The off-balance statue threatened to topple headfirst onto the road. The Egyptians ran around whipping the slaves, trying to get them to pull in the opposite direction to keep the statue from falling.

Whips cracked.

Slaves screamed.

Egyptians yelled.

All those people running around raised a cloud of dust that covered everything. The dust got in everyone's eyes, making it hard to see.

"Now's our chance!" Scarlett shouted to Sam. "Let's go!"

With all the noise and confusion and crowds of slaves scattering in all directions, no one noticed when Sam and Scarlett dropped their rope and ran. They were over the dunes and out of sight before the Egyptians knew they were gone.

***

"Now what?" Sam asked. "We might've given the Egyptians the slip, but we're still lost in the desert!"

His words rang all too true. The twins had been wandering around in circles since their escape. They were hungry, exhausted, and terribly thirsty—not to mention, in Sam's case, grumpy.

"Don't give up!" Scarlett said. "All we have to do is find Moses. We already know that he's here somewhere. Moses has God on his side. He won't let us down. He'll know what to do."

"Great! Just find Moses," Sam grumbled as he stumbled across the sand dune after his sister. "We only have to search through a zillion miles of desert. Where do you suggest we start looking?"

"How about here?"

Who said that? Sam and Scarlett turned around. They looked up.

And up.

And up.

Standing before them were two enormous men. They were built like basketball players— way taller and more muscular than any of the Egyptians the twins had seen. Instead of whips, they carried long, heavy sticks as thick as baseball bats.

"You said you were looking for Moses?" said

the taller of the two. "Well, you found him. I'm Moses."

"And I'm Aaron," said the other one in a booming voice. "Nice to meet you."

"We're brothers," they both said together.

"So are we," said Sam. "Well, not brothers. But we're twins. I'm Sam and this is Scarlett."

"You two aren't from around here, are you?" said Moses, raising an eyebrow at the twins' jeans and T-shirts.

"Not at all," said Sam. "In fact, we're hoping you can help us get back h—"

But before he could finish, Scarlett cut in. "Where are you guys going?" Scarlett asked Moses and Aaron.

"To Pithom," said Aaron, "to see Pharaoh. We're bringing him an important message from God. Pharaoh needs to listen to it."

"Unfortunately, he isn't such a good listener," added Moses. "And we don't have an appointment."

"Does that make a difference?" Sam asked.

Aaron and Moses grinned at each other. "Not to us!"

"I think I know what that message is," said Scarlett. "Pharaoh needs to set his slaves free."

"Good guess!" said Aaron, looking impressed.

"We'd like to help," Scarlett added. "Can we come with you?"

"Sure!" said Aaron. "Are you cool with snakes?"

"We're not scared of them, if that's what you mean," Scarlett said.

"My friend Omar has a pet corn snake," added Sam. "I've helped him feed it lots of times."

"Good! Then you can carry my staff," said Aaron. "Just don't drop it until I tell you. I don't want it getting away."

"How can a staff get away?" Sam asked. "And what does this have to do with snakes?"

Aaron laughed. "You'll see."

"What about me?" said Scarlett. "I want to help too."

"Great! You can both come," Moses said. "Aaron and I were just talking about how we weren't sure we could do this alone. Sam and Scarlett, you twins are just what we need!"

CHAPTER 6
PHARAOH'S PALACE

Sam and Scarlett followed Moses and Aaron across the desert. "When are we going to ask Moses to help us get home?" Sam whispered to Scarlett.

"Forget about that," said Scarlett. "Who wants to go home?"

"I do!" said Sam.

"Are you kidding me?" Scarlett said. "Here we are in ancient Egypt with Moses and Aaron. We're going to Pharaoh's palace so Moses can tell him to let the Hebrews go. This is going to be the most exciting event that ever happened, and we have a front-row seat. Moses even needs our help. We'll have a chance to be part of history. And you want to go home? Why? To do what? Play video games?"

"I wasn't thinking about video games," Sam said. "I was thinking that we were supposed to be helping with the Seder."

Scarlett grasped Sam by the shoulders. She looked into his eyes. "Sam, listen to me. If we don't help Moses, there isn't going to be a Seder. There isn't going to be a Passover. There isn't going to be an Exodus, because nobody's leaving Egypt!"

"I never thought about it that way," Sam said. "You're right. We need to help Moses free the slaves. When that's done, we'll see if he can get us back to our own time. Do you think everything will happen exactly like in the Haggadah?"

"Maybe not," said Scarlett. "After all, *we're* not

in the Haggadah. We might be able to change some things. Maybe we can even convince Pharaoh to let the slaves go right away—today!"

"I'd settle for getting out of this desert today," said Sam.

Moses turned around. "We're almost there," he said. "One more dune to go."

Sam and Scarlett followed Moses and Aaron up a tall sand dune. An astounding sight met them at the top. They saw the city of Pithom spread out before them.

Moses led the way into the city. Sam and Scarlett looked around in wonder. Everything in Pithom was new. The stone temples and monuments gleamed blinding white under the desert sun. The statues of gods and pharaohs were freshly painted. Hieroglyphs covered the walls.

"Can you read those hieroglyphs?" Scarlett asked Moses.

"Sure," Moses said. "*No littering. No loitering. No parking.*"

"The Egyptians have a lot of rules," said Scarlett.

"How can they have parking rules when there aren't any cars?" Sam asked.

"It means camels," Moses said.

"What are cars?" Aaron asked.

Sam didn't have time to answer. They had arrived at the royal palace.

***

Sam and Scarlett had never been inside a real palace, although they had seen plenty in movies, TV shows, and video games. Every fantasy story seemed to have a palace scene where the king gave the heroes an impossible task that usually involved dragons, monsters, or vampires.

Pharaoh's palace was nothing at all like those

fantasy palaces. It was more like an airport. Long lines and security guards were everywhere.

"At least we don't have to go through an X-ray machine," Scarlett whispered to Sam.

"We would if they'd been invented yet," Sam whispered back. They followed Moses and Aaron to the back of one of the lines.

"This won't work," Moses said. "We'll be here forever. We don't have any time to waste."

"Do you have a better idea?" Aaron asked. Sam and Scarlett were wondering the same thing. With all the security around, it wasn't like they could cut. But that was exactly what Moses had in mind.

"Follow me, guys," Moses said, leading them to the head of the line. A bald, well-dressed Egyptian stood in front, waiting his turn to see Pharaoh. He held what looked like a baby in his arms—a funny-looking baby! As Sam and Scarlett got closer, they saw it wasn't a baby at all. It was some kind of clay doll with a hippopotamus head.

"Excuse me, sir," said Scarlett. "What's up with the doll?" She had never been known to be shy.

"How dare you speak to me, slave!" the Egyptian shouted. "I am the high priest of the hippopotamus goddess Tauret. And how dare you call the sacred goddess Tauret a doll! Tauret and I came here today to see Pharaoh. Tauret has an important message for him. You have no right to cut in front of us. Get back to your places in line or you will feel the wrath of Tauret."

Then the doll spoke. *"Pay heed to the priest of Tauret. Obey—or Tauret will feed you to the crocodiles!"*

All the Egyptians waiting in line backed away, looking frightened. Sam and Scarlett tried hard not to laugh.

"That's not a goddess talking," Scarlett tried to explain to the Egyptians. "It's the priest. He's a ventriloquist—and not even a good one. Can't you see his lips move?"

The Egyptians were too frightened to listen. Besides, they clearly didn't know what a ventriloquist was.

"Tauret has spoken! You must obey!" they pleaded with Sam and Scarlett.

The doll suddenly spoke again. *"Tauret has changed her mind. Sam and Scarlett and their friends, Moses and Aaron, have an important message for Pharaoh. Tauret commands them to take first place in line. If you try to stop them, Tauret will feed you to the crocodiles!"*

The priest dropped his dummy. "It talks!"

"Surprised?" said Scarlett. The priest didn't seem to be listening. He was too busy running for the exit. He didn't even bother to take his dummy.

Scarlett picked up the hippo doll. She pulled the string at the back of its head to make its mouth open and shut. "Look," she told the Egyptians. "All these talking dummies, dolls, and statues are fake. You don't have to be afraid of them. Don't you see? They can't hurt you."

Scarlett felt Moses's hand on her shoulder. "Save it for later, Scarlett. These people aren't listening. They're too frightened."

"Moses is right," Aaron added. "And most people would rather believe in a god they can see. It's hard to believe in an invisible god. Even the Hebrews have a tough time with that."

"Next!" The guards summoned them into the throne room.

CHAPTER 7
STINKY

"How'd you do that?" Sam said to Scarlett as they followed the guards down a long corridor. "I didn't know you were a ventriloquist."

"I'm not," Scarlett said. "I just saw a video on YouTube once that taught you how to throw your voice. I didn't have to be very good. Just better than that Egyptian."

At the end of the corridor, the guards threw open two huge bronze doors. Sam and Scarlet found themselves in the presence of The Great and Mighty Pharaoh, Ruler of Upper and Lower Egypt and All the Lands Beyond. Everything about Pharaoh was awesome: his ten-foot throne, his enormous crown, the priceless jeweled rings and bracelets that covered his arms up to the elbows. Everything was overwhelming and awe-inspiring.

Except Pharaoh himself.

"Is that guy really the king of Egypt?" Scarlett whispered to Sam.

It was hard to believe that he was. Pharaoh looked like Mr. Grimes, their PE teacher. All he needed was a clipboard and a whistle.

"Bow down! On your knees!" Pharaoh commanded. He even sounded like Mr. Grimes telling everyone to get down and do ten push-ups. Sam and Scarlett didn't want to cause trouble for Moses or Aaron. Besides, bowing was easier than push-ups.

They were about to obey when Moses told them, "Stay where you are."

"They're supposed to bow," Pharaoh snapped. "I'm the pharaoh. Everybody has to do what I say. You too, Mose-Nose. Get down on your knees."

Moses remained standing. "Cut it out, Stinky. Did you forget that we grew up together? That we shared a bedroom? I'm happy to show you respect. But I'm not going to crawl around on the floor in front of your throne. I never did it before and I'm not doing it now. Anyway, we don't have time for this. I have an important message for you."

"And I have an important message for you. My way or the highway. You know where the exit is." Pharaoh glared at Moses.

"As a matter of fact, an exit is just what I'm here to talk about," said Moses.

"Too bad. I don't have time to talk to people who won't bow to me."

"Do they always carry on like this?" Scarlett whispered to Aaron.

"'Fraid so," Aaron said. "Moses and Stinky— that's Pharaoh—grew up together. Stinky's mom is Moses's stepmom. You see, when Moses was a baby, our sister Miriam put him in a basket..."

Scarlett finished the sentence. "And sent him floating on the Nile."

Aaron looked puzzled. "How do you know about that?"

Scarlett was about to say, "It's all in the Torah" until she realized there was no Torah. Not yet. There wouldn't be one until the Hebrews got out of Egypt and made it across the desert to Mount Sinai. Right now that didn't look as if it was going to happen anytime soon. So instead Scarlett said, "It's a famous story."

"I guess so," Aaron replied, not looking completely convinced. "Anyhow, Moses can be hard to live with. He's very bossy, always giving commandments. And Stinky—well, he's the king. All the Egyptians think he's a god. Everything he says is law. It's a bad mix."

"I can see that," Sam said. He wondered if he and Scarlett looked as bad as this when they started arguing. No wonder Grandma Mina lost patience. Maybe Moses and Pharaoh needed a Grandma Mina to call a time-out.

"Th-that's enough, Stinky," said Moses. "We're just w-w-wasting time."

"You started it!"

"D-d-d-did n-n-n-n-n-ot!" Moses sputtered.

"D-d-d-did t-t-t-t-too!" said Pharaoh, making fun of him.

"Wow!" Sam exclaimed. "This is just like that story Grandma Mina told us."

"What story?" Aaron asked.

"You know! The one when Moses was a baby and they brought him these two jars to see if he was going to be pharaoh when he grew up.

One jar held jewels. One was full of hot coals. Moses reached for the jewels, but the angels pushed his hand into the coals. A coal stuck to his finger and burned his mouth. That's why Moses stutters and why you have to speak for him."

"Huh? Who told you that?" Aaron said. "Moses's stepmom was the best mom in the world. She wouldn't let her baby near anything that might hurt him. Burning coals? Who makes up this stuff?"

"Never mind," Sam and Scarlett said together.

Just then Moses turned to Aaron. "You'd better t-t-take over. I c-c-can't get a word in edgew-w-wise."

"Right." Aaron stepped between Moses and Pharaoh. "Okay, Pharaoh, calm down. You and Moses will have to settle your issues between yourselves one day. Meanwhile, Moses and I have an important message to deliver to you."

"A message? From whom?" Pharaoh asked.

"F-f-f-f-f..." Moses tried to say something.

Aaron motioned for him to be silent. "From God," Aaron said.

CHAPTER 8

STAFF INTO SNAKE

Pharaoh started laughing. "Oh, of course, a message from God. That's what you told me the last time you were here. Is this message from the same god or from a different god? As you know, we have ten thousand gods here in Egypt. That's only the official ones. Every cat is a god—every crocodile, every hippo. There's a mouse god, a bird god, a snake god. You can't turn around without bumping into a god. And that's just the ones in Egypt. Nubia, Phoenicia, Babylon, Canaan, Assyria, and all the other lands have their own gods. So tell us, please, Aaron and Moses, which god has honored us with a message this time."

Pharaoh's laughter spread to the guards and courtiers. All the Egyptians in the throne room started laughing. Sam and Scarlett saw Moses shaking with anger.

"Th-th-th-th..." He stuttered so badly he couldn't get the words out.

Aaron took over. "There's only one God. God made heaven and earth. God rules the whole world. All other gods are fake—as fake as that hippo doll that Scarlett is holding. When the One True God talks, you'd better listen."

"And what would the One True God like to share with us today?" Pharaoh asked. Again, the whole court started laughing.

Moses whispered something in Aaron's ear. "God says," Aaron began, "that you're to give your Hebrew slaves a three-day holiday so that they can go to the desert and worship God in their own way."

"A holiday?" said Pharaoh. "Okay. But how do I know it's really God talking and not something you guys made up?"

"Show him, Sam," said Moses. This time he spoke in a loud, clear voice—without stuttering.

"Huh?" said Sam.

"You're holding Aaron's staff," said Scarlett. "You remember the story. You know what to do."

"Oh yeah!" Sam stepped forward. "Okay, Stinky—I mean Pharaoh. You think we're making this up? Watch this!" Sam struck the end of the heavy staff on the floor and let it go. The wooden rod began to twist and turn. As Sam and Scarlett watched, it turned into a snake.

A garter snake.

"That's it?" Sam cried. "A garter snake? An ordinary little garter snake?"

"Just wait," said Moses.

Pharaoh was chuckling. "Is this what you had to show us? Come on, Mose-Nose! That's the best your god can do? Even my apprentice magicians can do better than that. Show him, boys!"

At least two dozen Egyptians came forward. They were dressed in white linen. Their bodies were completely shaved. They didn't even have eyebrows. While Moses's staff was just a wooden stick, the magicians' staffs were made from ivory, silver, and bronze. They were inlaid with jewels and crowned at the top with gold images of Egyptian gods.

Pharaoh's magicians threw their staffs on the floor. The staffs began to wriggle. Then squirm. Then slither. And they grew and grew until they turned into huge snakes the size of pythons.

"Uh-oh!" Sam said to Scarlett. "I think Aaron just lost his staff."

"Not quite," said Scarlett. "Look!"

One by one, the little garter snake grabbed the magicians' snakes and swallowed them whole. The last one disappeared down the little green snake's throat like a piece of spaghetti. Sam picked up the snake by the tail. Once again, it became a staff—except that it was even heavier and thicker than it had been before. Sam could hardly lift it.

"Nice work, Sam," Aaron said.

Moses turned to Pharaoh. This time he didn't stutter. "Well? You just saw a little bit of God's power. Give the Hebrews time off so they can go to the desert to worship God in their own way. Three days. That's all I ask. And then we'll come back."

"No," Pharaoh said.

"Why not?" said Moses.

"Because I'm Pharaoh. Who cares what your stupid snake does? I'm Number One here. What I say goes. And what I say is NO! Can you hear me, Mose-Nose? No! No! No!"

Moses began sputtering and stammering.

Aaron turned to Sam and Scarlett. "They're starting in again. This could go on for a while. Why don't you kids find a nice, quiet place to sit and relax? I'll come find you when it's time to leave."

"Sure, Aaron," Scarlett said. She turned to Sam. "Where should we go?"

"You don't suppose there's a Starbucks around?" said Sam.

"No, but there's probably a garden somewhere," Scarlett said. "It would be nice to sit in a garden— smelling the flowers, listening to the water splashing in the fountains."

"Yeah," said Sam. "Especially after that awful desert. Maybe there'll be a swimming pool."

"Let's find out," said Scarlett.

CHAPTER 9
SETI

Sam and Scarlett slipped out through a side door. "Which way?" Scarlett asked Sam.

"Your guess is as good as mine," said Sam. The corridors of Pharaoh's palace were like the mazes in a crossword puzzle book. They branched off, doubled back, led to dead ends. Worse, there were no arrows showing which direction to go. And while there were plenty of hieroglyphs on the walls, Sam and Scarlett couldn't read them.

Finally, Scarlett stopped a servant who was racing down the hall with a bowl of dates. "Excuse me. We're looking for a garden..."

The servant couldn't pause to answer. He pointed behind him, down the hall.

"Let's go," said Scarlett, leading the way.

Sam glanced back over his shoulder. "Those dates looked good. I'm sure he could've spared a couple. We should've asked him."

"You're right," Scarlett said. "I can't remember the last time we ate anything. I'm so hungry I could eat this hippo doll. Maybe we'll find something to eat in the garden."

"If we ever get there," said Sam.

The halls and corridors kept branching off. The twins stopped along the way to ask directions from a troop of soldiers, two scribes, a man who was sweeping the hallway, and finally an artist on a scaffold who was chiseling hieroglyphs into the wall.

"What do those hieroglyphs say?" Scarlett asked the artist.

"*This Way to the Garden*," he told her. "It's straight ahead."

Sam and Scarlett gave each other a high five and raced down the hall.

But what they found wasn't quite what they'd been expecting. The end of the hallway opened onto some kind of patio. Walls surrounded it, but there was no roof. The top was open to the sky. There were even two structures at opposite ends that looked like basketball hoops, except that they were made of stone.

Even stranger, a young man at the far end was bouncing something that definitely looked like a basketball. The young man's skin was golden brown like his hair, which was braided into cornrows and finished with blue and gold beads. He wore a kind of pleated kilt that looked like a pair of basketball shorts. His feet were bare, but playing on the hard stone surface of the court didn't seem to bother him. Every now and then he'd take a shot at one of the hoops. He got it in nearly every time, except once when it rolled off the rim.

"This is really strange," said Scarlett. "I didn't know they had basketball in ancient Egypt."

"Let's find out what's going on," Sam said. He walked over to the young man shooting the ball. "Hi!" he said, holding out his hand. "I'm Sam. And this is my sister, Scarlett. Want to play a little one-on-one?"

"Sure!" the young man said. "How about if your sister plays too? It'll be two-on-one, but that's fair because I'm taller."

"Yeah, but we're better," Sam said.

"You're on, dude! By the way, I'm Seti." He tossed the ball to Scarlett.

"Nice to meet you, Seti," said Scarlett. "We're gonna beat you."

"We'll see about that!"

Scarlett started dribbling. Seti blocked. Not only was he tall—he had long arms. Getting by him would be a challenge. Scarlett passed to Sam. Sam began a drive toward the basket while Scarlett came in from the opposite side. Seti was tall, but he had to keep his eyes on both of them. Sam passed to Scarlett. Scarlett pretended she was going to shoot. As soon as Seti blocked her, she passed to Sam, who drove in for the basket.

"Nice!" Seti exclaimed, taking hold of the ball. He turned and sank a three-pointer from center court. *Swish!* The ball went right through the hoop.

"Wow!" said Sam. "Awesome shot!"

"Thanks. You guys are pretty good yourselves. I've got the height, that's all."

"You've got more than that," said Scarlett. Sure enough, as they kept playing, Seti proved he was a much better player than Sam or Scarlett could ever hope to be. He could sink a ball from anywhere on the court with his eyes closed. But as good as he was, he didn't show off. Most of the time he played a passing-blocking game with Scarlett and Sam so they could keep up with him. There was a lot of running. Add the desert heat, and Sam and Scarlett were soon out of breath.

"I need a break," panted Sam. Sweat rolled off his face as if someone had sprayed him with a hose. Scarlett felt just as wrung out.

"I'm ready for a break too," Seti said. He pressed a recess in the wall. A section of the wall's stone slid aside, opening the way to a garden filled with roses.

"So that's where they keep the garden! Who could ever find it?" Scarlett said.

"It must be a private garden, like those special lounges at the airport where you need a card to get in," said Sam.

Scarlett and Sam followed Seti into the garden. They flopped down in the shade of a palm tree. A splashing fountain cooled the desert breeze, which carried the scent of the roses. In the distance, beyond the garden wall, the twins could see boats with brightly colored sails going up and down the river.

"Is that the Nile?" Sam asked.

"What else would it be?" Seti answered. "I guess you guys aren't from around here."

"You might say that," said Sam. He wondered how he could explain where he and Scarlett were from and how they had gotten to Egypt. Fortunately, Scarlett changed the subject before Seti had a chance to ask.

"This is beautiful!" Scarlett said. "Grandma Mina would love it. She adores roses."

"I love roses too," Seti said. "So does my dad. So do most Egyptians. You've probably noticed that Egypt is mostly desert. Everything is dusty brown. I guess that's why we love bright colors."

"Is your dad the gardener?" Sam asked.

Seti laughed. "Not quite."

"What does he do?" said Scarlett.

Seti looked embarrassed. "Well, I don't like to brag about it."

"It's cool," Sam assured him. "Just tell us!"

"My dad's . . . Pharaoh."

The twins gasped. "You're kidding," said Sam.

Scarlett couldn't believe it either. "How can your dad be Pharaoh? You're so nice and he's so . . ." She didn't want to finish, but Sam did.

". . . awful! We just came from the throne room. We were there with Moses and Aaron. Pharaoh was yelling at Moses and making fun of him and not paying attention to anything he was trying to say. If Pharaoh has his way, the Hebrews will be slaves in Egypt forever."

Seti looked more disappointed than angry. Sam suddenly wished he hadn't pushed Seti about what his dad did for a living. He should have just assumed Seti's dad was a gardener and left it at that.

"Sorry, Seti," said Scarlett. "You've been really great to us. We shouldn't be talking trash about your dad."

"Yeah," said Sam. "I didn't mean to hurt your feelings."

Seti sat down underneath the palm tree between Sam and Scarlett. "How about some snacks?" he asked, changing the subject.

"Sure!" Scarlett said.

"So you're not mad at us?" asked Sam.

"For talking that way about my dad? How can I be mad when it's true? He can be a jerk sometimes. Nobody knows that better than I do."

Seti rang a bell hanging from the palm tree. A door in the wall opened. Two servants entered the garden, carrying a jug and several baskets. They took a carpet from one of the baskets and spread it beneath the tree. The second basket was full of fruit, cakes, cups, and dishes, which the servants laid out on the carpet. They filled the cups with reddish juice from the jug. Then, as silently as they'd come, they bowed and disappeared back through the secret door in the wall.

"Try some of this," Seti said, handing cups to Sam and Scarlett.

"Hey, this is good!" Sam said. "All of a sudden I don't feel so wiped out. Is this some kind of energy drink?"

"I guess you can call it that," Seti said. "We call it *wu-ren-hem-mat.*"

"What does that mean?" Scarlett asked.

"Energy drink," said Seti with a shrug. "We also invented *hat-rem-nus-war.*"

"What's that?" asked Sam.

"It's the game we just played," said Seti. "Throw the Ball in the Basket."

"You invented basketball?" said Sam. "Wow, you Egyptians are pretty smart."

"In some ways," Seti said. "Not so smart

in others."

Scarlett finished her drink and put her cup back on the table. "How so?" she asked.

Seti sighed. "Well, take my dad for instance. You're right about the way he acts. If all I knew about him was what I saw in the throne room, I'd think he was pretty awful too. But he's not. Not all the time. He's a great dad when we're alone together. We play sports, go fishing. He taught me how to shoot arrows, how to drive a chariot. He loves to tell jokes. He even does magic tricks. I wish I could show you my favorite. It's where Dad takes a stick and turns it into a snake..."

"I think we've seen that one," said Sam.

"But explain something to me, Seti," said Scarlett. "If your dad is so great when you're alone—and I believe he is—why does he act like such a jerk in public?"

"It's because when we're together—just the two of us—he's Dad. When he's on the throne, he's

Pharaoh. And that's a whole different story."

"I still don't get it," said Scarlett.

"Me neither," said Sam.

"It's like this," Seti explained. "Pharaoh is supposed to be special. He's supposed to be the god-king of Egypt. People worship Pharaoh as one of the gods. So Dad feels he has to be a god. That means he has to be right all the time. He can never admit he made a mistake. He can never ask for advice. He can never change his mind. Once he's made a decision, he has to stick with it, even when it's clear to him and everyone else that it's wrong."

"Eesh! It must be hard to live like that," said Scarlett.

"It is. Believe me!" said Seti. "What's worse is that since he's a god, Dad can't have any friends. Everyone has to bow down to him. Everyone has to be scared of him. And he has to make sure they stay scared. He does that by being cruel. That's why Dad and Uncle Moses can't get along. Moses isn't fooled by Dad's Scary God-King act. He knows what Dad's really like. In fact, I think Moses really loves Dad."

"Then how come Moses calls your dad Stinky?" Sam asked.

"So what?" said Seti. "Dad calls him Mose-Nose. It doesn't mean anything. It's what siblings do."

"Yeah," Sam and Scarlett said together, thinking of all the names they had called each other.

"What Uncle Moses can't stand is the guy Dad becomes when he sits on the throne," Seti continued. "It doesn't have to be this way. I've told him a hundred times. 'Dad, relax! Be yourself. You don't have to be right all the time. You can admit you've made mistakes. It's okay to be kind and merciful. The people of Egypt will still respect you. They'll obey you out of love, not fear.' But he can't see it. And Egypt's running out of time."

"What do you mean?" Sam asked.

"Egypt's going broke," Seti said. "We can't afford to keep building these new cities and pyramids. And the priests! They're the worst. They're always telling my dad, 'The hippo god wants a new temple.' So then we have to build them another temple, even though they just got a new one three years before. And if the hippo god gets a new temple, then the crocodile god and the jackal god and the cat god and all the other gods need a new one too. Our people have to pay for the building materials with taxes. The Hebrews had to become slaves because we couldn't afford to pay anyone to do all that hard work."

"What would you do if you were the pharaoh, Seti?" Scarlett asked.

Seti poured himself some more energy drink. "I'd start by freeing all our slaves. Slavery is cruel. It's also stupid. How can you expect people to do any work if you beat them all the time and don't feed them? And having to find straw to make bricks after you've been working all day? That's crazy! I'd free everyone who wanted to leave Egypt. And I'd pay real wages to anyone who wanted to stay. I'd get rid of the whips and fire the cruel overseers. I'd also tell the priests not to expect any more temples. They'll have to live with what they have."

Seti paused, then added in a lower voice, "Between you and me, I'm not convinced these animals are really gods. Maybe a cat is just a cat."

"Who do you think God is?" Sam asked.

Seti thought for several minutes before answering. Sam and Scarlett could tell this was a question he had been thinking about for a long time.

"A long time ago we had a pharaoh called Akhenaten. He believed there was only one god, the Sun, who ruled over heaven and earth. I believe Akhenaten was right. We don't need all these expensive temples and fancy ceremonies.

The sun's light shines everywhere and on everyone. That's the kind of god I believe in."

"Wow!" Sam whispered to Scarlett. "I wish Seti was the pharaoh instead of his dad."

"If Seti was the pharaoh, we wouldn't be here," Scarlett answered. "The Hebrews wouldn't be slaves. They could leave Egypt any time they wanted."

"But he's not the pharaoh," said Sam.

"No." Scarlett sighed. "We still have a ways to go. Want to shoot some more hoops?" she asked Seti.

"Sure!" Seti said.

Their second game had just gotten started when Aaron showed up. "There you are!" he said to Sam and Scarlett. "I've been looking all over for you."

"How's it going, Uncle Aaron?" said Seti.

"Not great," said Aaron. "Sorry to interrupt your fun, guys, but we need to leave. Now."

"Did it get ugly?" Seti asked.

Aaron nodded. "I think you'd better get in there and calm your dad down."

Seti shook his head. "I'll do what I can. Where's Uncle Moses?"

"He stormed outside and told me to meet him by the river as soon as I rounded up these two. Sam, Scarlett, let's go. Moses said to hurry."

The twins said good-bye to Seti. "We'll be back," said Scarlett.

"I hope so," Seti said. "We have to finish our game."

Sam and Scarlett followed Aaron down the maze of corridors. They could still hear Pharaoh's enraged screaming as they hurried through the palace gate.

CHAPTER 10
PODCAST

"This is Sam."

"And I'm Scarlett. We decided to tell this part of the story as a podcast. We're recording it on my cell phone. I think I have enough battery left, but let's not waste any time. We're broadcasting live from ancient Egypt. Here's what's going on. Take it, Sam!"

Sam

Thanks, Scarlett! After we left the palace, we found Moses waiting for us by the Nile. We expected him to be angry. Instead, he looked sadder than anyone I ever saw.

"That Stinky!" he kept saying. "Why is he so stubborn? Can't he see what a horrible mistake he's made?"

We remembered what Seti told us. "Maybe he can," I said. "He just won't admit that he's wrong."

Scarlett

And I added, "He's too stubborn to admit that there's a God more powerful than Pharaoh—a God more powerful than all the gods of Egypt put together."

"You're right," Moses said. "What makes me sad is that the Egyptian people will have to suffer for his attitude. Because now I must do what God tells me. It breaks my heart, but I have to obey."

Sam

Moses whispered in Aaron's ear. Aaron nodded and walked down the riverbank with his staff— the same one I'd been holding for him earlier. He whirled the staff above his head. Then *SMACK!* He brought it down on the water with a big splash.

I got some water on my face. No big deal. Except suddenly I heard Scarlett yell, "Sam, what did you do to yourself?"

I reached up to touch my face. My fingers were covered with sticky red stuff. Blood! Was I bleeding? How did that happen? Nothing had hit me. I hadn't bumped into anything.

"He's fine," said Moses. "He's just got a mild case of the plague."

That's when I figured it out. The blood didn't come from me. It came from the Nile River. When Aaron smacked the river with his staff, all the water in the Nile turned into blood. That's what splashed on my face.

Scarlett

It was a relief to know that Sam wasn't hurt. His face looked like he'd been in a car wreck. After we got him cleaned up, Moses and Aaron took us to their home in the land of Goshen, where all the Hebrews live. It was getting late, and we didn't have anywhere else to stay.

Sam

Moses and Aaron introduced us to their parents, Amram and Jochebed, who told us to make ourselves at home. Their sister, Miriam, got us settled.

Scarlett

Wow! Miriam is really something! I hope I'm just like her when I grow up. You can tell who's boss in this family. As soon as we walked in, Miriam had Aaron setting the table and Moses chopping up vegetables. Sam, does Miriam remind you of anyone?

Sam

Yeah! How about Grandma Mina? I guess that's good that Miriam's so used to taking charge, because if she hadn't thought of putting Moses in the reed basket when he was a baby and stayed around to see what happened to him, we might all still be slaves in Egypt.

Scarlett

Double yuck to that! Anyhow, while Sam and I were getting to know Moses's family, every drop of water in Egypt had turned into blood.

Sam

The water in the canals turned to blood. So did the water in the wells. Water in jars and cups turned to blood. All the fish in the Nile died.

Scarlett

The water in the temple pools turned to blood.

The crocodile god and the hippo god couldn't do anything about it. They crawled out of their pools and hid under the awnings. There wasn't one drop of water to be found in the whole land of Egypt.

Sam

The Egyptians were dying of thirst. They couldn't even drink their own spit. Scarlett and I couldn't help worrying about Seti. We told ourselves that maybe this plague didn't affect energy drinks. Deep down, we knew it did.

Of course, none of this affected the Hebrews. We had plenty of water. But when we tried to give some to one of the poor Egyptians, it turned to blood.

Scarlett

That was the worst part—seeing all those people suffering and not being able to help them. Even all the way over in Goshen, we could hear the Egyptians' groans and cries. It was horrible. But we knew the drill: the plague would only end if Pharaoh agreed to free the slaves.

Sam

And what did Pharaoh do? Nothing. He said turning water into blood was no big deal. His magicians could do it too. Yeah, right!

Scarlett

Moses gave him seven days to think it over. Then we all went back to the palace to see if Pharaoh had changed his mind. No way! So God decided it was time to raise the stakes.

Sam

God told Moses to have Aaron take his staff and stretch out his hand over the land of Egypt. I wish we had taken a video to show what happened next. Frogs came swarming out of the Nile and every pond, lake, canal, and well in Egypt. There were gazillions of them! All those frogs croaking at once could make you deaf. The racket went on day and night.

Scarlett

And they got into everything. Seti told us that you'd hop into bed and about two dozen frogs would hop out. You'd open a drawer or a box: frogs! You'd bite into a loaf of bread and you'd find a frog baked in it. Or worse—half a frog.

Sam

And if you stepped on them, they didn't just squish. They'd explode! *Pow!* It was like walking on land mines. You'd be covered with frog goo.

And with so many frogs all over the place, it was impossible not to step on some. Even if you could avoid them, they had this nasty habit of jumping in front of you just as you were about to put your foot down. *KA-POW!* Frog everywhere!

Scarlett

But in the land of Goshen, we didn't have a problem. There wasn't a frog in sight.

Sam

The Egyptians started screaming at Pharaoh to do something. He was supposed to be the god-king of Egypt, right? What kind of god-king lets a bunch of frogs take over his kingdom?

Scarlett

Pharaoh called Moses and Aaron and told them the Hebrews could go to the desert. Fine. The frogs died all at once. But once the frogs were dead, Pharaoh changed his mind.

Sam

That still left the frogs, though. There were huge, smelly heaps of dead frogs all over Egypt. They brought in a zillion flies, and they stank. Pharaoh didn't care. He figured he'd won that round.

Scarlett

Not quite. The next plague was lice. I know—what's the big deal about a few lice? They're everywhere. They can show up on anyone.

Not like this.

The first Egyptians I saw looked like they were wearing weird gray leotards. They kept waving their arms, jumping up and down, scratching like crazy. It wasn't until I got closer that I realized the leotards were moving. The Egyptians were covered with a living carpet of lice.

They scraped off lice by the handful. They rolled in the dust. They jumped in the river. They doused themselves with every kind of medicine the priests and doctors could come up with. Nothing worked.

But just like the frogs, there were no lice on the Hebrews. Fleas, yes. Mosquitoes and spiders, yes. Ants too. But not one louse could be found in the whole land of Goshen.

Sam

It was the same routine again. Pharaoh promised to let the Hebrews go. But once the lice were gone, so was the promise. So God sent another plague: wild beasts.

Scarlett

That's what they call it in the Torah. I think it's because words for these kinds of animals didn't exist at that time. We know what to call them now.

Dinosaurs.

Sam

Scarlett isn't kidding. The first ones came out of the desert. When I saw an apatosaurus peeking over a pyramid, I thought I needed glasses—or Scarlett and I had traveled even farther back in time. Turns out the dinos were the time travelers that day, not us. Next a triceratops showed up, just walking down the street in the middle of the day. It must have been hungry, because it stopped at a fruit stand and ate everything in it—the stand too! You should've seen the Egyptians run.

Scarlett

Those guys were lucky. Triceratops wasn't a meateater. But tyrannosaurus was. I saw a T. rex chasing a group of Egyptians down the street. I recognized one of them. It was the Egyptian who was in charge of the slaves when Sam and I were in the desert. I guess that's why I didn't feel too sorry when the T. rex tossed him in the air and gobbled him down like a peanut.

Sam

Dinosaurs started coming out of the Nile too. A plesiosaur stuck its long neck out of the water. It plucked the crocodile god out of its pool in front of the crocodile temple and ate it. You could see the bulge in the plesiosaur's neck as that huge crocodile went down, down, down until it disappeared. Then it swam to the next temple and finished off the hippo god for dessert. By this time, the priests were running to the palace, pleading with Pharaoh to do something.

Scarlett

Same story. Over and over again. Pharaoh promises. Pharaoh goes back on his promise. Sam and I were getting tired of walking back and forth to the palace with Moses and Aaron. The only bright spot was getting to hang with Seti while Moses told Pharaoh to let the Hebrews go and Pharaoh told Moses it wasn't going to happen.

We could see that the plagues were getting Seti down. He felt bad not only for himself but for all the Egyptians. He said that when his dad wasn't in the throne room, he just went into his bedroom and closed the curtains so he wouldn't have to see his people suffer.

Sam

So the plagues kept coming. All the animals died, including the god-animals in the temples. This scared the Egyptians more than anything. If their gods couldn't protect themselves, how could they protect anyone else?

Scarlett

Boils came after that. The Egyptians were covered with sores that oozed black pus. It smelled and attracted flies. Seti told us each boil felt like being stuck with a hot needle. Luckily, he only had a couple. I don't know if Pharaoh got any! He acted as if he didn't, or if he did, they didn't bother him.

Sam

Yeah, but I noticed he wasn't sitting on his throne when we went to see him. I bet he had a few boils where he sat.

Scarlett

Then came hail. The smallest hailstones were the size of softballs. The biggest ones were as large as SUVs. They flattened the crops in the fields and smashed buildings. I saw a pyramid collapse. One hailstone even knocked off the Sphinx's nose.

Sam

Next up, locusts. I never saw so many grasshoppers in my life. They ate every blade of grass, every green leaf in Egypt. Then they started on the temples. They had eaten through the woodwork and were gnawing on the stone when Pharaoh called it quits.

Scarlett

That lasted about ten seconds. Time for the next plague. This was the deepest darkness you can imagine. It was like being in a cave a mile belowground and turning off your flashlight. It wasn't that the light was dim. There was no light!

Nobody could see anything. The Egyptians stumbled around in the darkness. Being superstitious, they imagined all kinds of demons and evil spirits stalking around—not to mention thieves. They panicked at the slightest noise. Whole families would start punching each other out because they couldn't see whom they were fighting. What a nightmare!

Sam

At least it didn't last long. Pharaoh sent for Moses right away. I still don't know how the messenger found our house. No light came from anywhere—not even the moon or the stars. Maybe God allowed him to have a little light so he wouldn't get lost.

Getting to the palace was easy for us, though. We had plenty of light along the way. It was as if a giant flashlight shined its beam on us as we went through the streets. All around, we could hear Egyptians moaning and groaning, tripping over things, knocking into each other, bumping into walls. A few even stumbled into our circle of light. I wondered why they still couldn't see anything. But they couldn't. The only answer we could think of was that it was just like all the other plagues. The Egyptians suffered plenty, but the Hebrews weren't affected.

Scarlett

When we got to the palace, we were surprised to see there were no guards. I guess they got lost in the darkness. Our miracle light led the way to Pharaoh's throne room. Pharaoh sat on his throne, all alone in that empty space. He couldn't see us, but we could see him. He looked like he'd been crying.

"I've had it, Mose-Nose!" he yelled into the darkness. "Take your Hebrews and leave Egypt. Now! Don't ever come back."

He sounded as if he really meant it this time.

Sam

Right on cue, the darkness lifted. It was like somebody had just flipped a light switch. Pharaoh spent a few seconds blinking.

Moses asked, "So do we still have a deal?"

Pharaoh squinted at him. "You heard what I said. Get out of here."

We all let out a long sigh of relief. "Thank you, Stinky," Moses said. "I'm sorry you had to go through all this. Tell Mom I said good-bye. Maybe I'll see you again someday."

"Not if I see you first," Pharaoh said.

Scarlett

We ran into Seti as we were leaving the palace. He looked exhausted and depressed. He hadn't slept or eaten much in the past few days. Sam and I each gave him a big hug.

"I guess this is good-bye," I said. "The Hebrews are leaving Egypt. Your dad gave us permission. For real. Finally."

"Yeah? That's great," Seti said. But he didn't look as happy as we expected. We asked him what was wrong.

"I don't know," he said. "I have this feeling that something bad is going to happen. Really, really bad."

"No, it won't," I told Seti. "We're leaving Egypt. Everything's going to be fine from now on."

"I hope you're right," said Seti.

So did we.

CHAPTER 11
COUNTDOWN

"Hey, you two! That's enough! You need to get busy." It was Miriam calling out to the twins.

"We're just winding up our podcast," Scarlett said.

"Looks like fooling around to me. I need both of you now. There's a lot of work to do and not a lot of time to do it."

"Sure! We'll help," Scarlett said. "We're running out of battery anyway. What do you want us to do?"

Miriam took a moment to go over her mental checklist. "Moses is packing up the camel. Aaron went to get a lamb. I guess the two of you can get started baking bread."

"How do you bake bread?" asked Sam. "Isn't it a big deal?"

"You've never baked bread before? I can't believe it! Two strong kids muddling around with modcasts—whatever that is—and you don't even know how to bake bread?"

"Well, we don't have to bake it. Mom buys it at the supermarket," said Sam.

"What's a supermarket?" Miriam asked.

"Never mind, Miriam," Scarlett said. "Teach us what we have to do and we'll do it."

Miriam told Scarlett and Sam to follow her. She led them outside to a pit covered with flat stones. A fire burned underneath. A large clay pot held something that looked like pale pudding. Scarlett guessed it was dough. A covered basket stood next to it.

"Watch me. I'm only going to show you once," said Miriam. Sam and Scarlett sat down on the ground next to her so they could see what she was doing. "You pick out a lump of dough. Then you pat it between your hands, back and forth, like this. You want to make it flat, thin, and round. Now you lay it on the stones. When the edges turn brown and the top starts to bubble, use this stick to turn it over on the other side. Give it a few more minutes. Then pull it off the stones and put it in that basket. Now you try it."

"Aren't you supposed to use yeast or some kind of leavening?" Sam asked. "Don't you have to give the bread time to rise?"

"Since when do you know about bread?" Scarlett demanded.

"Food Channel," said Sam.

"I don't know about any Food Canal," said Miriam. "If you want food, you have to make it yourself. You're right about leavening, Sam. That's what we usually do. But not now. There isn't time. Just throw the dough on the stones, cook it, pack it, and start on the next one."

"What do you mean, there isn't time?" asked Sam.

"Well, if you two had been paying attention instead of talking into that shiny rock of yours, you would've heard the news. Pharaoh canceled his promise. Again."

Sam and Scarlett groaned. "So we're staying in Egypt after all?" asked Scarlett.

"Nope," said Miriam. "We're making a run for it. We leave tonight. We're not asking Pharaoh's permission this time. And there's nothing he can do about it. So we need to make as much bread as possible before we hit the road. Let's see you try it."

Neither Sam nor Scarlett accomplished much with their first efforts. Their bread was misshapen

and lumpy—burned on the outside and raw in the middle. Sam dropped his as he took it off the stones. That made it burned, raw, and sandy.

He tore off a piece to taste. "Ugh! This reminds me of bad matzah."

"Because it *is* matzah, Sam!" Scarlett hissed, so that Miriam wouldn't hear. "Can't you see what's happening?"

"What, we're baking bad matzah? It doesn't take a genius to see that."

"No! Don't you get it? We're baking the *original* matzah. It's Pesach! The very first one. And we're here. We're part of it. "

"Whoa!" said Sam as he lifted another piece of bread from the stones. "You're right, that is pretty cool—OW! I just burned my fingers!"

That's when Aaron came around the corner of the house, holding a bleating lamb on his shoulders. "How's the bread coming?" he asked. He picked up a piece and took a bite. "It needs something."

"Yeah—leavening," Miriam said. "You take what you can get."

"Well, keep plugging away, guys," Aaron said as he walked off with the lamb. "We're going to need every crumb."

"That lamb is cute. Where's Aaron taking it?" Scarlett asked Miriam.

"You don't really want to know, do you?" said Miriam.

"Uh...never mind," said Scarlett. Sam gulped.

The twins quickly got back to their baking. They were getting into a rhythm now. Sam was good at patting the dough flat and thin. Scarlett had an eye for pulling the bread off the hot stones at just the right time. The whole process didn't take more than a couple of minutes.

"Looking good!" said Miriam. "If you two don't need me, I'll start working on dinner. Moses gave me a list. Salt water, eggs, parsley, lettuce, horseradish. Where am I going to get horseradish? Am I supposed to pull it out of the air? Those two brothers of mine drive me crazy sometimes!"

Miriam walked away, still muttering to herself.

"Wait a minute," said Sam, as he and Scarlett kept turning out unleavened bread. "I thought the lamb was for dinner. Why does Miriam need all that other food?"

"The lamb's not for dinner, Sam! It's for the first Passover sacrifice. Remember?"

"Oh, yeah. To ward off the last plague. But we're done with the plagues, aren't we?"

"Do the count, Sam," Scarlett said. "We're one short." She ticked them off on her fingers. "Blood-Frogs-Lice ..."

Sam continued. "Wild beasts ... Sick animals ... Boils ..."

"Hail ... Locusts ... Darkness. That's nine," said Scarlett.

"You're right," Sam said. "We've got one plague

to go. Which one was that?" Sam began counting off the plagues again. He held out his little finger and dipped it in the air as if he were dipping drops of wine out of his cup at the Seder table. *"Dam ... Tzfardeah ... Kinim ..."*

"Stop counting. I just remembered what the last plague is. It's the scariest plague of all." Scarlett suddenly looked pale.

"What is it? What's wrong?" Sam asked. Then he remembered. *"Makat Bechorot.* The Death of the Firstborn." He shivered.

"That means the oldest son of every family in Egypt is about to die," said Scarlett. "Including ..." Her voice trailed off.

"I suddenly don't like the look of this," said Sam.

"We've got to do something," said Scarlett. "Seti's our friend. He's Egypt's future king. And he'll be a great king. We can't let anything happen to him."

"Okay," said Sam. "We need a plan. What if we find Seti and bring him back here? He'll be safe with us in the middle of all the Hebrews. And when the coast is clear, he can be pharaoh and the rest of us can leave Egypt."

"That's so simple it just might work," said Scarlett. "But Miriam won't let us go to the palace when there's so much to do here. And we can't tell her we already know what's going to happen. She'd ask too many questions."

"Then we'll do just what we did when we needed to get away from the Egyptians," said Sam. "We'll wait for a chance to sneak out. Everybody's rushing around, loading up the animals, herding the sheep, taking care of last-minute stuff. We'll slip away, find Seti, and bring him back here while everyone's too distracted to notice."

"You're a genius, Sam!" Scarlett exclaimed. "Let's hurry up and finish this baking."

CHAPTER 12
THE TENTH PLAGUE

Sam and Scarlett set to work. By now they had the process down. They worked as a team, not wasting a second. Sam slapped out the unleavened cakes. Scarlett flung them on the hot stones, turned them, and flipped them off. The sun was beginning to go down over the Great Pyramid by the time they finished baking the last of the dough. They wrapped the bread in linen and packed it into baskets for the journey. Mission accomplished.

Just as they were about to slip out of the house to find Seti, Moses came in. He was carrying two brushes and a wooden pail filled with what looked like red paint. "Sam and Scarlett, are you done with the bread?" he asked.

"It's all squared away," Sam answered.

"Good. I have an important job for you. I want you to take this pail and walk around the neighborhood. Make sure every house has the sign painted on its doorway."

"What sign?" Scarlett asked.

"This!" Moses dipped a brush in the pail. "Come on. I'll show you. I was just about to do ours." Moses painted a smear on each doorpost and a third on the lintel over the doorway. The red liquid dripped down.

"Cheap paint," said Sam.

"It's not paint," Scarlett whispered. "Remember the lamb?"

Sam's face turned pale. "You mean that's ..."

"Blood," said Moses. "The blood of the lamb that we will eat tonight for our feast. It will be the last meal we eat in Egypt. God has spoken. We leave tonight. But every Hebrew house must have that special mark on its doorway. Some people will forget. Some are old or sick and can't do it themselves. Others may not have saved the blood from the sacrifice. We have to help each other. If you see a doorway that doesn't have the right sign, paint it on."

"Why?" asked Sam. "What's going to happen?" The twins knew the answer, but they wanted to hear what Moses would say. Did he know that his own nephew, Seti, was in danger?

"The last plague is coming," was all Moses said. "Can I count on you to stand with me, no matter what happens?"

"We won't let you down, Moses," Sam and Scarlett said together.

"I knew that as soon as we met," said Moses.

"Go now. Hurry. When you finish, come join us at the feast."

***

Sam and Scarlett rushed down the narrow alleys between the Hebrew houses. They checked every door. There wasn't much for them to do. Most doors already had the special sign: three telltale splashes of blood on the lintel and on the doorposts. The light began to fade as the sun went down. People started gathering for the evening meal: the first feast of Passover.

"I just thought of something. How can you have a Seder without a Haggadah?" Sam wondered.

"They'll figure it out," said Scarlett. "I think we're done here. All the doors have the sign. Let's bag this and find Seti."

"I'm with you," said Sam. They ditched the pail

and the brushes in someone's backyard. Then they made a run for the palace.

Sam and Scarlett noticed the change as soon as they left Goshen. There, the moon and the stars shined down. Here, where the Egyptians lived, the sky was black as if covered by an angry cloud. The Hebrew homes were bright with joyous feasting. The Egyptian homes were dark and silent. The streets were empty. The twins heard no animal noises. Not even a cat crossed their path.

"This is creepy," said Sam. "Let's find Seti fast so we can get out of here."

They hurried to the palace. Even in the darkness they were in no danger of getting lost. They'd come here so many times with Moses and Aaron that they could find their way backwards.

But this time something was different.
Very different.

Sam grabbed Scarlett's arm. "Look, Scarlett! Slow down. There's a guard at the gate."

"So what? There's always a guard. We'll tell him we have an urgent message for Pharaoh. He'll let us through. They always do. They all know who we are by now."

"This one's different. Take a good look at him, Scarlett. A good look."

Scarlett paused. She and Sam ducked behind a statue and peered at the guard. Sam was right. This was no ordinary Egyptian soldier. There was nothing ordinary about him. He wasn't even human.

He was extremely tall—twice the height of Seti. His head wasn't a man's head at all. It was the head of an eagle, covered with shining golden feathers that glowed in the darkness. Instead of a nose or a mouth, he had an eagle's beak. His eyes were the yellow eyes of a bird of prey. On his shoulders were two great eagle's wings. His feet were the clawed talons of a raptor. But he wasn't completely a bird. He had a human body, although his skin was covered with scales like a reptile. He stood with his two muscular arms crossing his chest, looking like a wrestler waiting for the match to begin.

"What *is* that?" Scarlett whispered.

"Maybe it's one of the Egyptian gods come to life," said Sam. "They have a lot of weird-looking gods—half-human, half-animal."

"Can't be," said Scarlett. "The Egyptian gods don't exist. They may be paintings or statues, but they never were real. This guy is very real."

"It doesn't matter who he is. We just need to find a way to get by him so we can get into the palace and find Seti."

"Any ideas?"

"Yeah!" Sam picked up a stone. "I'll throw this rock to distract him. When he leaves the gate to see what made that noise, we'll run for it. Ready. One ... two ..."

Sam had a good arm. He often pitched on

his after-school baseball team. The stone flew into the darkness. It clattered on the pavement, several yards from the gate. The eagle guardian turned its head.

Sam and Scarlett ran for the gate.

"Stop!"

Four more eagle-faced guards appeared out of the darkness to bar their way. Two others came behind them. They were trapped.

"Get out of our way!" Scarlett shouted at them. "You have no power over us. We don't believe in you. You're not gods. You aren't even real."

"We are not gods." The creatures spoke as one. Their voices sounded as if they were generated by a computer. They moved as if they were characters in a video game. Sam wondered if they were supposed to blast their way through. How? They didn't have any weapons. Not even digital ones.

"If you aren't gods, who are you?" Sam demanded.

"We are messengers," the creatures answered. "You may know us by another name: *malakhim.*"

"Angels!" Scarlett whispered. "That's what *malakhim* means—messengers from God."

"If you're supposed to be messengers, what's the message?" Sam asked the angels.

"Go back! This is not your place. You do not belong here. You belong with the Hebrews and all the other slaves who are leaving Egypt this night."

"Fine," said Sam. "We'll go back...as soon as we find our friend Seti. He's going with us."

"He cannot," the angels said.

"Why not?"

"Because he was Pharaoh's firstborn son. Seti is dead, along with all the other firstborn sons of Egypt."

Sam and Scarlett gasped in horror. Above their heads they heard the sound of giant wings, as if a huge bird were flying through the night sky. Then silence. But only for a moment. A scream followed, so deep and vast it sounded as if the very stones of Egypt were wailing. Agonized cries came from the streets, the houses, the rooftops. But the loudest, most heartbreaking wails of all came from Pharaoh's palace.

As the cries swelled, the *malakhim* disappeared, like bad guys in a video game when they get zapped. The way into the palace was open.

But Sam and Scarlett knew they would find nothing there. "Don't cry, Scarlett," Sam said, though he was crying himself. "We can't do anything here. The Passover feast must be almost finished. Moses and the others are going to need us more than ever."

It was time to take their place with the Hebrew people. The Going Out from Egypt was about to begin.

CHAPTER 13
LEAVING EGYPT

Getting back to Goshen turned out to be much easier, and at the same time much harder, than they ever imagined. Although Egyptians filled the streets, not one tried to stop the twins. Their hearts were too full of sorrow to bother with a couple of strangers.

"My baby! My baby! Oh, my dear little boy!"

"My brother is dead!"

"Husband, how could you leave me? What will

become of us without you?"

An old man sat on his doorstep with his head on his knees, moaning, while the woman beside him sobbed. People wandered around in a daze, so crushed by grief that they no longer knew or cared where they were going. Once-elegant women sat in the street, pouring dust on their heads.

All of Egypt was in mourning for its lost children. Sam and Scarlett mourned with them.

"I can't believe Seti's dead," Scarlett choked out through her tears. "Why did this happen, Sam? Seti was so good. He would have made a wonderful king."

"I don't know the answer," Sam said. "Maybe Moses will know. There must be an explanation."

"I don't care if there is one," said Scarlett. "Seti's gone. There's nothing anyone can do about it now. I want to leave this horrible place. This minute!"

"Then let's keep moving," said Sam.

***

Sam and Scarlett made their way through the Egyptian crowds until they reached Goshen.

Here too crowds of people filled the streets. The Passover feast had ended, but no one rejoiced. They had heard the terrifying wings flapping above their houses in the dead of night. They heard the wails and cries coming from their Egyptian neighbors. They trembled as they realized that only a splash of lamb's blood on their doors had kept them safe.

Dawn was breaking over the pyramids. It was time to leave. All belongings were packed into bags and bundles. Families gathered in the streets with their sheep and goats, their camels and donkeys, their dogs and cats.

"Looks like we're just in time," said Sam. "The journey's about to start."

"Journey to where?" demanded an old man

standing nearby. "To a Promised Land none of us have ever seen? How do we know it even exists? And even if it's real, how will we get there? If you ask me, Moses hasn't thought this through at all."

The old man wasn't the only one with doubts. Scores of people had gathered around Moses, shouting questions and demanding answers. Moses was doing his best to calm everyone down, but his stutter was tripping him up. As soon as he saw Scarlett and Sam, he ditched the Q&A session and pushed his way through the crowd to get to them. His strong arms scooped both of them into a hug.

"Where were you? Aaron and Miriam didn't know where you had gone. I was frantic. We couldn't start our journey from Egypt without you. Where did you go?"

"To Pharaoh's palace," Scarlett answered. "We tried to save Seti." She couldn't say any more.

"I know," Moses said quietly. "Remember, Seti wasn't just Pharaoh's son. He was my nephew.

I loved him. I grieve for him too. He was a fine young man. He would've made a great pharaoh."

"Why did it happen, Moses?" Sam demanded. "You talk to God. You must know why. Why did Seti have to die when God let Stinky live?"

"We should never wish harm to any human being, Sam," said Moses. "But when God spoke to me in the desert, God said, 'I am Who I am.' God does what God does. There is always a reason, though it may be beyond our understanding." Moses looked from Scarlett's tearstained face to Sam's. "I know that's not the answer you were hoping for. But we don't always have answers. All we have is our faith that God's actions are just and right. We have to trust God, even when it's hard."

Sam and Scarlett glanced at each other, then back at Moses. Slowly, Sam nodded. Scarlett started to wipe her eyes.

Just then, Aaron rushed over to Moses.

"They're getting impatient," he said. "What should we tell them?"

Moses whispered in Aaron's ear for a long moment. Then Aaron nodded and turned to the crowd of Hebrews. "Listen up, all of you! We know that you're worried about the future. But God will never abandon us. God will protect us on our journey. We can overcome any obstacle in our path as long as God is with us."

Murmurs of approval rippled through the crowd.

Moses took a deep breath. "Are you r-r-ready to leave Egypt?" he asked them.

"Yes!" they answered with one voice.

"Then l-l-let's go!" Moses pointed his staff down the road they were to take. At once the entire nation began to move—not only the Hebrews but slaves of other nations who wanted to be free. They all started their journey together. People called to each other in Hebrew,

Canaanite, Philistine, and a host of other languages. Camels roared. Donkeys brayed.

In the midst of the noise and confusion, Sam and Scarlett saw an amazing sight. A gigantic elephant with huge ears and enormous tusks made its way through the crowd. An equally gigantic, dark-skinned African man sat on the elephant's shoulders. He pressed his feet against the elephant's ears to steer the animal through the narrow streets. Then he raised his arms in the air and cried, "Thank you, God of Israel! I am free! I am free!"

The elephant, as if he understood, raised his trunk and trumpeted with joy.

Moses called up to the man. "Juba! I have a special job for you. I want you to bring up the rear. Make sure everyone keeps up. No stragglers! I don't want anyone left behind."

Juba answered with a sigh. "Am I to be the last to leave Egypt? I wanted to be the first. Well, the

God of Israel has spoken. I will obey. We all play our part. Even Tusker."

"Who's Tusker?" Scarlett asked.

"That's the elephant," Moses said. He called up to Juba. "I have one more favor to ask. This one comes from me, not God. Would you take my two friends with you? I want them to see everything. They'll have the best view from up there."

"Indeed they will!" Juba said. "Well, you two? What are you waiting for? Come on up!"

"I don't see a ladder," said Sam.

"You don't need a ladder," Juba called down to him. "Take hold of Tusker's trunk. Tusker will pull you up."

"I'm not so sure about this," Sam told Scarlett.

"If Moses wants us to do it, it must be okay," said Scarlett. "I'll go first." As she approached Tusker, the elephant curled the end of his trunk into a ball. Scarlett stepped on it and held on. Tusker lifted her high into the air. Juba caught her hand and pulled

her behind him onto Tusker's back.

"How is it?" Sam called to her.

"It's so high up!" said Scarlett. "It's a little scary, but not bad. It's kind of exciting,"

"Of course it's exciting," said Juba. "Do you get to ride an elephant every day? Come, boy! Your turn."

Tusker lowered his trunk and lifted Sam. "Wow!" Sam said as he found his place behind Scarlett and Juba. "I can see all of Egypt from up here!"

"That is true," Juba said. "But my joy will come when I see Egypt no more."

CHAPTER 14
JUBA

Bringing up the rear of a vast exodus was not easy. People always lagged behind for different reasons. Tusker used his great strength to right carts that had tipped over and pick up loads that had fallen off. Sam and Scarlett often got down to help parents find lost children and to help children find lost pets. Stubborn camels and donkeys that suddenly decided to stop had to be persuaded to keep moving. Tusker was good at that.

All the while Juba kept looking back over his shoulder.

"Why do you keep looking back? I thought you wanted to see the last of Egypt," Scarlett asked him.

"I do," Juba said. "I am looking back in case Egypt follows us." Sam and Scarlett didn't know what to say to that.

As Tusker walked along the road leading out of Egypt, Juba told Sam and Scarlett his story.

***

Juba

I come from Nubia. That is a land that lies south of Egypt along the River Nile. My father was elephant master to Nubia's king. I grew up with elephants. Elephants are very smart. Do you know that they have their own language? Elephants are like brothers and sisters to me, especially Tusker.

We are the exact same age.

I was a young man when the Egyptians invaded our country. They thought they had the right to make the Nubians their slaves because they were more powerful. Our army fought back. But after many battles, we were defeated. Tusker and I became prisoners. Fortunately for us, Pharaoh wanted Tusker as a pet for his menagerie. The great beast would only obey me, so I became Tusker's keeper. We had an easier time than the other Nubian prisoners. Pharaoh turned them into slaves, just as he did with the Hebrews. The Egyptians treated them just as cruelly. Few are alive today.

Moses was a little boy then. He came to the elephant house every morning to play with Tusker. Tusker liked Moses. He wouldn't let any other Egyptian order him around, but he'd do whatever Moses asked.

When Moses grew up, he got in some trouble and had to leave Egypt. Tusker and I missed him.

I often wondered what happened to him. Then, not long ago, he returned. He told us he had been living in the desert. There God spoke to him out of a bush that burned with fire. God sent him back here so he could lead the Hebrew slaves out of Egypt.

"I'm happy for that," I said. "But it does me little good. I am not a Hebrew. I'll be a slave to Pharaoh until the day I die."

"Not so!" Moses told me. "God will free you too. And Tusker. He will free all the slaves in Egypt."

"How can that be?" I asked.

Moses answered, "The God of Israel is not the god of one people. God rules the universe. All people are his children. God cares for all of them. God hears and answers their prayers. God will set you free, Juba. You must believe it."

I thought long and hard about what Moses said. We have many gods in Nubia. But above them all is the Great God who rules the heavens.

I thought to myself, "Maybe the God of Moses is the same Great God we worship in Nubia. There is no need to worship all the little gods if the Great God is my friend. From now on I will only worship the Great God."

The Great God heard my prayers. God protected us from the terrible plagues that struck the Egyptians. Tusker and I are both eldest sons. But as you see, we are both still alive. God saved us. God freed us. I will worship the Great God, the God of Moses, forever. So will Tusker, in his own elephant way.

***

Slowly the great procession covered mile after dusty mile. Moses and Aaron walked in the lead. Miriam and her friends came next. They danced, sang, and played tambourines to keep up everyone's spirits. If people needed to rest, Tusker lifted them onto his back. Sam and Scarlett sometimes had to get down and walk to make room. What mattered most was that everyone kept moving.

The first day passed. That night the group camped at an oasis along the way. Sam and Scarlett drew water from the well for Tusker. He sure drank a lot! Juba shared his food with them. Sitting beside the campfire, Sam and Scarlett looked up at the stars through the leaves of the date palms. The campfires of the people leaving Egypt filled the desert night. They seemed as numerous as the stars themselves.

People began singing and dancing. Only now— after they had put miles between themselves and the Egyptians—could they truly begin to feel free.

Only Juba seemed worried. "What's the matter?" Scarlett asked him.

"I'm not sure where Moses is leading us. We need to turn north to cross the border into the desert," Juba said. "This way leads to the Red Sea. Surely Moses is not taking us to the sea. How will we get across?"

Sam and Scarlett knew the answer to that, but they weren't going to tell. How could they? No one would believe them. Meanwhile, Juba got more and more worried. Especially at noon the next day, when the sparkling waves of the sea appeared in the distance.

Everyone stopped. High on Juba's back, Sam, Scarlett, and Juba saw crowds of people flopping down to rest near the seashore.

"Why are we not moving?" cried Juba. "We can't stay here." Tusker paced back and forth, swinging his trunk. They could tell that he was getting nervous too

"Everything will be all right, Juba," Sam tried to tell him. "You'll see. Moses knows what he's doing."

"I hope so," Juba said. He glanced back over

his shoulder. "Oh no!" he exclaimed.

"What's wrong?" Scarlett asked.

Juba pointed to a dust cloud in the distance. "Chariots."

CHAPTER 15
AT THE SEA

Panic began spreading through the crowd.

"Chariots are coming!"

"It's Pharaoh's army!"

"They're moving fast..."

"We'll never outrun them."

"We're doomed!"

"No, we're not!" Sam called out. "Don't worry, everything will be fine!"

"No one seems convinced," said Scarlett as the

chaos continued.

"Can you blame them?" asked Juba. "Think how angry the Egyptians must be. Their sons are dead. They've been tormented with plagues. We left their country, and now they realize that they will have to do all the work themselves. If we are lucky, they will make us slaves again. If we are not..." Juba's voice trailed off.

"What?" asked Scarlett.

"We are trapped here between the Egyptians and the sea. None of us are soldiers. Tusker's trumpeting may hold them off for a while. Horses are afraid of elephants. But there is only one Tusker. He cannot hold off the Egyptians forever. My guess is that Pharaoh will drive us into the sea and let us all drown. Then he will tell his people, 'See where their god led them!'"

"But if we get across the sea before Pharaoh's army gets here, we'll be fine," Sam pointed out.

"Get across the sea? How? Do you see any

boats?" Juba shook his head hopelessly. "It would take a miracle." Tusker swung his head back and forth, sharing his master's despair.

"Then we'll just have to come up with a miracle," said Scarlett. "Let us down, Juba. Sam and I need to talk to Moses."

Sam and Scarlett slid down Tusker's trunk to the ground. They wove their way through the crowds until they came to the seashore. Moses and Aaron stood at the water's edge, surrounded by an angry swarm of Hebrews who were getting angrier by the minute.

"What now, Moses? Tell us what we're supposed to do! You led us here!"

Moses was stuttering worse than ever. "T-t-t-t-t-t..."

"Trust in God," Aaron translated. "God brought us out of Egypt. God will show us the way." Furious shouts drowned out his voice.

"We should've stayed in Egypt! At least

Pharaoh gave us food. He didn't bring us out here to die in the desert. Or to drown in the sea!"

"You w-w-won't d-d-d-rown in the s-s-sea," Moses tried to tell them. "The s-s-sea w-w-w-will open f-f-for you. B-b-b-behold the p p p power of G-G-G-God!" Moses stretched his staff over the waves. Nothing. The surf rolled over his sandals.

"Huh?" said Sam. "This isn't how the story goes."

"Something's wrong," said Scarlett. "Why isn't the sea parting?"

"Maybe someone needs to shout louder," Sam suggested. "You try, Aaron."

Aaron took Moses's staff, stretched it out over the sea, and called in a voice like thunder, "BEHOLD THE POWER OF GOD!"

Still nothing. A few people laughed bitterly. Others began to wail. "Surely God didn't bring us here to die! What are we going to do? Save us, Moses!"

Sam and Scarlett looked at each other. "This is bad," said Sam.

"Moses needs help," Scarlett agreed. "We know what's supposed to happen. We have to figure out why it isn't happening and come up with a way to *make* it happen."

"If Moses can't do it, how can we?" asked Sam.

"I have an idea," said Scarlett. "Remember how Grandma Mina always says that miracles happen to those who believe in them? If you want God to work miracles for you, you have to believe that miracles can happen."

"Okay," said Sam. "I believe. Now what?"

"We walk into the water. And keep walking. And trust God, like Moses said."

"Just walk into the sea?"

"Yup," said Scarlett. "That should be all it takes."

"I hope you're right. Anyway, it's the only plan we've got." Sam tugged on Moses's sleeve to get his attention. "Moses, we need to start walking into the sea. All of us. I promise God won't let us down."

"You're our leader," added Scarlett. "You have to go first."

"I c-c-can't," Moses said.

"Why not? You're the bravest man I know!" Sam said. He could see Moses trembling.

"I'm ... afraid of water. I don't know how to swim."

"Neither do I," added Aaron. "Nobody in Egypt does. The Nile River is full of crocodiles."

"You don't have to know how to swim," said Scarlett. "And you don't have to worry about crocodiles."

"You floated down the Nile River in a basket when you were a baby," Sam reminded Moses. "And God kept you safe."

"I know," said Moses. Then he glanced at Miriam. "But I had some human help too."

"Don't look at me," said Miriam. "I stayed on the shore." She turned to Sam and Scarlett. "You two will have to show us what to do."

"There's nothing to it," said Scarlett. "We'll do it together."

Scarlett took Moses's hand. Moses took Sam's. Sam took Aaron's. Aaron took Miriam's. Together, they all walked into the sea.

"Behold the power of God!" Moses called out, stutter-free at last.

The sea began to open like a zipper. The water piled up on two sides, leaving a pathway down the middle that went all the way to the opposite shore.

"You and Sam have worked a miracle!" Moses told Scarlett.

"No," Scarlett said. "Anyone could have done it. All you needed was faith."

"And a few swimming lessons didn't hurt," Sam added.

"A miracle! A miracle!" the people cried.

"What are you waiting for?" Aaron called back to them. "God just opened the sea for us! Let's go!"

CHAPTER 16

HORSE AND RIDER

The people marched between the waters, following Moses, Miriam, and Aaron to the other side of the sea. Sam and Scarlett stayed behind. They waited until they saw Tusker and Juba.

"Is anyone behind you?" Sam shouted to Juba.

"No. We're the last. We need to hurry. Those chariots are traveling fast. We must all get to the other side of the sea before they arrive." Tusker didn't take time to stop. He lowered his trunk and swept Sam and Scarlett onto his back. They held tight to Juba as the great elephant lumbered onto the seafloor.

What incredible sights! Sam and Scarlett could look through the water and see what lay at the bottom of the sea as clearly as if they were visiting an aquarium. They saw sunken ships. A lost city. Strange-looking fishes. Scarlett spotted an open treasure chest with emeralds and pearls pouring out onto the sand. Each gem was the size of a baseball. But there was no stopping to gather souvenirs. Tusker hurried along as fast as an elephant could go.

"We made it!" shouted Sam as Tusker climbed up from the seabed. The elephant stood on the sand, breathing hard. That didn't stop him from raising his trunk and trumpeting with joy.

Moses, Aaron, and Miriam rushed over to greet Juba and the twins. "Our God came through, Moses," Juba cried. "I will never doubt God again."

"Don't speak too soon," said Miriam. "We're not safe yet."

She was right. The path through the sea still lay open. Chariots were approaching the opposite shore. Pharaoh's chariot rode in the lead.

"Did you think you could get away?" Sam and Scarlett heard Pharaoh shouting. "I'll haul you all back to Egypt. Every one of you! If you think you worked hard before, that'll seem like vacation compared to what I have waiting for you! You'll curse Moses and his god every day you find yourselves alive. That won't be long—if you're lucky!"

"Go back, Stinky! Don't do it! Please!" Moses cried.

Did Pharaoh hear him? Even if he did, would it have made any difference? Pharaoh and his chariots raced down the path between the waters. Sam and Scarlett saw it happen. The towering walls of water began to tremble. Then, with a rush, they poured in. In a single moment the path, the horses, the chariots disappeared beneath the sea. Sam and Scarlett watched the seagulls flying above the waves as if nothing had ever happened.

Moses stood alone at the edge of the sand and wept. "My brother... poor Stinky. His whole army. All those soldiers. Even those beautiful horses. Why wouldn't he listen?"

"It's not your fault," said Scarlett, taking his hand. "You gave him every chance."

"What more could you have done?" asked Sam.

"I know you two are right," said Moses. "But I can't help it. He was my brother. I feel so sad."

"Of course you do," said Miriam. "But now isn't the time for sadness. God has delivered us from Egypt. We've got to rejoice, Moses." Miriam raised her tambourine and called out to the people. "We are safe. We are free. Pharaoh can never trouble us again. This is the greatest miracle of all! Come on, everybody! It's time to celebrate!"

Everyone on the seashore began singing with Miriam. Aaron, Moses, Sam, Scarlett, and Juba joined in. Even Tusker trumpeted along.

"I will sing to God, for God is great.

Horse and rider God threw into the sea…"

"Sam, look! What's that over there?" Scarlett pointed to a colorful object lying on the sand.

"It's Grandma Mina's carpet!" Sam cried. "How did it get here?"

"Who knows?" Scarlett said. "Well, we can't leave it behind. We'll roll it up and carry it with us." But as soon as the twins touched the carpet's edges, something strange began to happen.

"I can hear everybody singing, but their voices are getting faint," said Scarlett. "It's like somebody turned down the volume."

"Same here," Sam said. "And everything's getting fuzzy. It's starting to fade…"

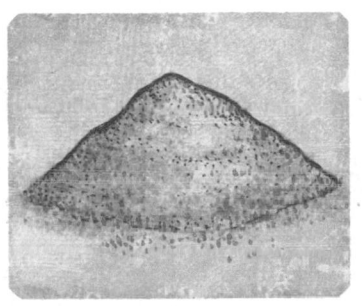

CHAPTER 17

FOUR QUESTIONS

Suddenly everything became clear again. But now Sam and Scarlett were no longer at the shores of the sea. They were home, sitting around the Seder table. They saw Dad and Mom and Grandma Mina. They saw the Seder plate and the three covered matzot and the glasses of wine.

Grandma Mina's carpet hung on the wall— with a small pile of sand on the floor beneath it. Sam and Scarlett looked at Grandma Mina. She winked. They all shared the secret.

"Let's not take all night," said Dad. "Who's going to ask the Four Questions?"

Sam and Scarlett glanced at each other. After all they'd been through, the fight they'd had earlier seemed ridiculous. "We'll do it together."

They began. *"Mah nishtanah ha'laylah ha'zeh mi'kol ha'laylot*—why is this night different from all other nights?"

Then they both laughed. How was it different? Where should they begin?

The Story of Passover

The first Passover happened long ago in Egypt.
The story is told in the book of Exodus in the
Torah. A cruel king, Pharaoh, ruled over Egypt.
He was worried that the Jewish people would
rise up and fight against him, so he decided
to make them his slaves. They were forced to
work from morning till night making bricks
and building palaces and cities. In their despair,
the Jewish people asked God for help, and God
chose a man named Moses to lead them.

Moses told Pharaoh that God was not happy

with the way Pharaoh was treating the Jewish people and that God wanted them to leave Egypt and be free. But Pharaoh refused. That is when the Ten Plagues began to happen to the Egyptians. First, the water of the Nile River turned to blood, so the people could not drink. Next came hordes of frogs filling their houses. Later, wild animals attacked them. Huge balls of hail fell from the sky, and locusts destroyed the fields and ate the Egyptians' food.

Each time a new plague began, Pharaoh would cry, "Moses, I will let the Jewish people go. Just stop this horrible plague!" Yet no sooner would God take away the plague than Pharaoh would shout, "No, I've changed my mind. The Jews must stay!" So God sent more plagues.

Finally, after the tenth plague, Pharaoh ordered the Jews to leave Egypt.

Fearful that Pharaoh might again change his mind, the Jewish people had to pack quickly to leave Egypt. They didn't have time to prepare food or allow their dough to rise into bread. They had only enough time to make a flat, cracker-like bread called matzah. They hastily tied the matzah to their backs along with their other possessions and left their homes with Moses leading the way.

The people had not traveled far before Pharaoh once again changed his mind and commanded his army to bring the Jews back to Egypt. But the Jews continued to flee, stopping only when they reached the large, stormy sea. The Israelites had no boats. What could they do? They prayed! God heard their prayers, and a miracle happened. The sea opened up, forming two walls of water with a dry, sandy path between them. The Jews hurried down the path and across the sea. Just as they reached the other side, the walls of water closed and the path disappeared. The sea separated the Jews from the land of Egypt. The Jews were free!

Each year at Passover, we eat special foods, sing songs, tell stories, and participate in a Seder—a special meal that helps us remember the miraculous journey from slavery to freedom.